Margie and Wolf

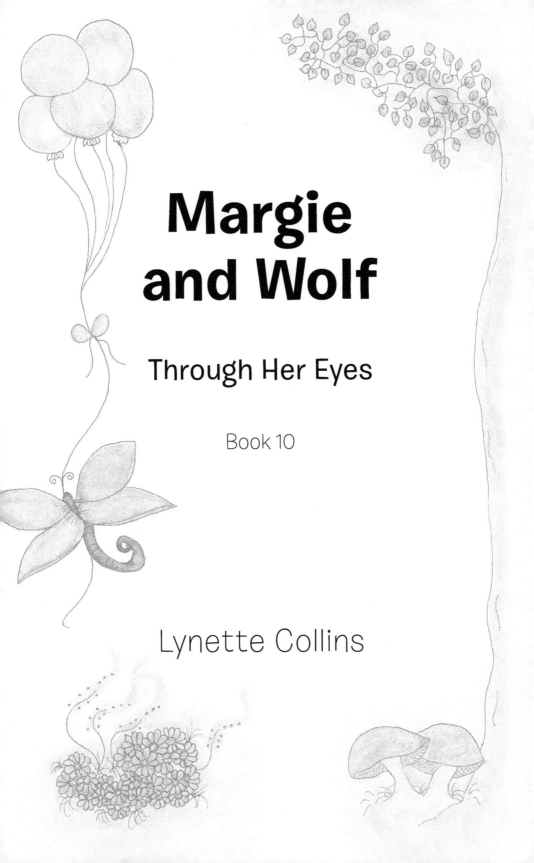

Margie and Wolf

Through Her Eyes

Book 10

Lynette Collins

Rev. date:03/30/2019

To order additional copies of this book, contact:
Xlibris
1-800-455-039
www.Xlibris.com.au
Orders@Xlibris.com.au
792373

As the sun came up, Blueberry knew it was going to be a great day.

Blueberry said to her Mother, 'I am going to play with Margie and Wolf. We are going back to my old bush next to the stream to say hello to my old friends.'

Miss Poisonberry said, 'That would be fine, but I want you home by dark.'

'Yes, Mother,' Blueberry replied.

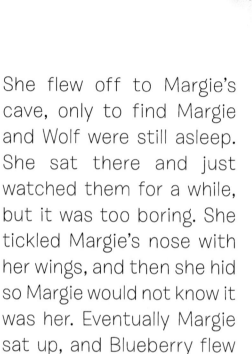

She flew off to Margie's cave, only to find Margie and Wolf were still asleep. She sat there and just watched them for a while, but it was too boring. She tickled Margie's nose with her wings, and then she hid so Margie would not know it was her. Eventually Margie sat up, and Blueberry flew up to Margie's face, with a cheeky grin.

'Oh, Margie, you're awake? It's a beautiful day. Would you like to go to the meadow's?'

'Yes, that sounds like a good idea,' said Margie. She rubbed her eyes and scratched her nose as she looked around.

Blueberry asked, 'What are you looking for?'

'Oh, I felt like something was tickling my nose, but it must have been a dream.'

Blueberry laughed and nodded. 'Hmm... it must have been.'

They made their way out of the cave, and Margie went for a quick swim before starting her day. When she got out, Margie's mother had a freshly opened coconut ready for her for breakfast. Margie said thank you to her mother, and told her she was taking Blueberry to the meadows to play.

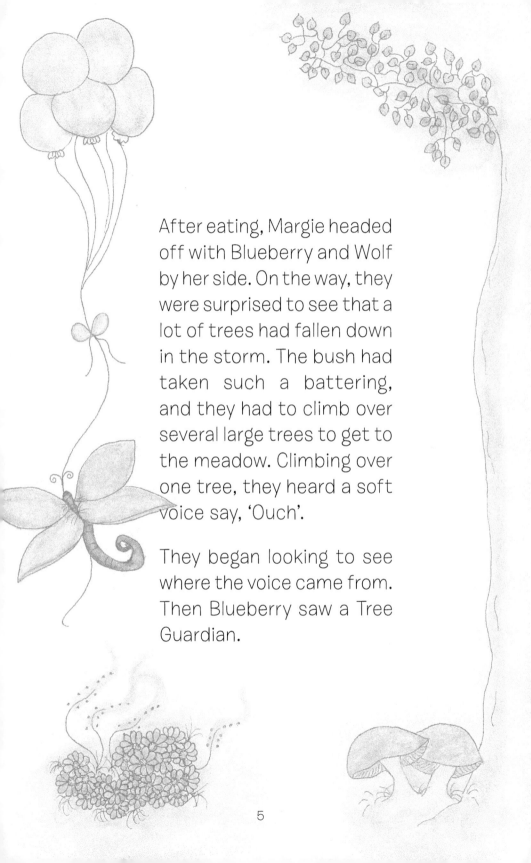

After eating, Margie headed off with Blueberry and Wolf by her side. On the way, they were surprised to see that a lot of trees had fallen down in the storm. The bush had taken such a battering, and they had to climb over several large trees to get to the meadow. Climbing over one tree, they heard a soft voice say, 'Ouch'.

They began looking to see where the voice came from. Then Blueberry saw a Tree Guardian.

'Hello, are you stuck?' said Blueberry.

Margie and Wolf looked on in amazement; they didn't know that such a creature existed.

'Where do you come from?' Margie asked.

Blueberry said, 'They come from the trees, silly! Have you never seen a Tree Guardian before?'

'No,' both Margie and Wolf said, at the same time.

'Would you be able to pick this rock up off my leg?' asked the Tree Guardian.

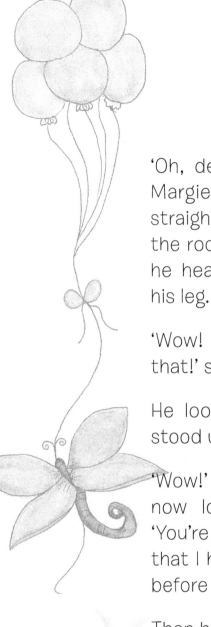

'Oh, dear! I am so sorry,' Margie said, and walked straight over and removed the rock, then watched as he healed a deep cut on his leg.

'Wow! I wish I could do that!' said Margie.

He looked at Margie and stood up.

'Wow!' Margie said again, now looking up at him, 'You're very tall! How is it that I have never seen you before now?'

Then he disappeared.

Margie asked, 'Where did he go?'

Blueberry said, 'He is right here.'

Margie and Wolf looked around.

Margie said, 'Stop playing tricks on us, Blueberry.'

'I am not. You know how the fairy makes you invisible to danger?'

'Well, yes,' Margie replied.

'They also make Tree Guardians invisible to humans,' said Blueberry.

'Oh,' Margie said, 'so you're right here, huh?'

Margie put out her hands to touch him, and he reappeared once again.

Blueberry asked, 'What's your name?'

He replied, 'My name is Terrain.'

'Oh, what a nice name,' Margie replied, as Terrain began to blush.

Blueberry asked, 'Where are your parents?'

'Well, I don't know. We all got separated in the storm. The tree that we were in got blown over, for it was quite an old tree.'

He walked up to their tree and called, 'Momma, where are you?'

When there was no answer, as he sat down on one of the branches, and began to worry.

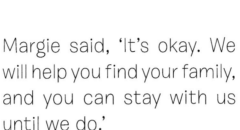

Margie said, 'It's okay. We will help you find your family, and you can stay with us until we do.'

Terrain looked at Margie and said, 'You're such a good helper to all that lives in the bush, Margie.'

Wolf whimpered and Terrain said, 'and you, Wolf.'

'I often see you two helping the others. I just never thought I would be one of those that need of your help,' said Terrain.

Margie said, 'You have seen us before?'

'Oh, yes,' Terrain replied, 'we are always watching! That's what we do. My mom and sisters love you, for you have such a beautiful heart, and we like it when you sing. We call your tribe the salt water people.'

'Oh,' Margie replied, 'so how many sisters do you have, Terrain?'

'I have two.'

Margie asked, 'Is there more family like yours living in the bush? I mean more Tree Guardians?'

'Oh, yes! We are the only ones around here, but deep in the bush there are lots of us.'

'Wow! Are they all as tall as you?'

'Yes, but my mom and father are very tall indeed.'

Terrain then saw his mom and began running up and called out, 'Momma, I thought I had lost you!'

Margie and Wolf could not see anyone there. Then Terrain told his family that Margie, Wolf and Blueberry helped him, and then the Tree Guardian family all appeared in front of Margie and Wolf.

'Wow! You're right,' Wolf said, 'your parents are very tall!'

They all laughed, and Terrain's Momma thanked them for helping Terrain and looking after him.

Terrain's sisters said, 'Hello, Margie.'

Margie asked, 'What are your names?'

Terrain's mom said, 'My name is Tempest, and my husband's name is Basalt, and this is Keenly and Indigo.'

'Well, nice to meet you all,' Margie, Wolf and Blueberry replied.

Indigo asked, 'Next time you play tag, can we play too?'

'Of course, you can. We were going to play today, but it's getting later now, and we have to be back before dark, but we will meet you in the meadows tomorrow, and we will all play,' Margie replied.

'Yes!' The girls clapped.

Then Margie, Wolf and Blueberry began to head back home. They were waving goodbye when they were amazed to see Terrain and his sister climbing the trees right to the top.

Margie called out, 'Don't fall,' as Terrain jumped from the top of the tree.

Margie screamed and then out came Terrain's beautiful big wings, and he laughed at her.

Margie said, 'That was not funny, Terrain!' and began running home.

When bedtime came, Margie cuddled up with her family, ready to go to sleep. Then she asked her Mother about the Tree Guardians.

Her grandfather said, 'There is no such thing.'

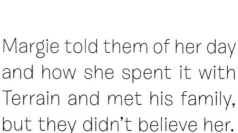

Margie told them of her day and how she spent it with Terrain and met his family, but they didn't believe her.

Margie's Mother said, 'You have a beautiful imagination, and I love how it's so wild with a new friend. I love you Margie. Good night.'

Margie said, 'But, Mother, it's true!'

Then Father said, 'That's enough. If there were Tree Guardians, we would know of them. It's time to go to sleep. Good night, family.'

Margie was sad that no one believed her.

'But Mother...' she began.

Mother said, 'Enough, go to sleep now.'

Margie looked up at Wolf, as he covered his eyes with his paws and went to sleep. Margie looked up at the top of the cave and gazed at the fire beetles. She started to think about tomorrow and how she could not wait to see her new friends again.

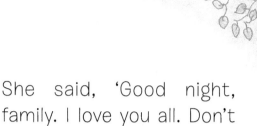

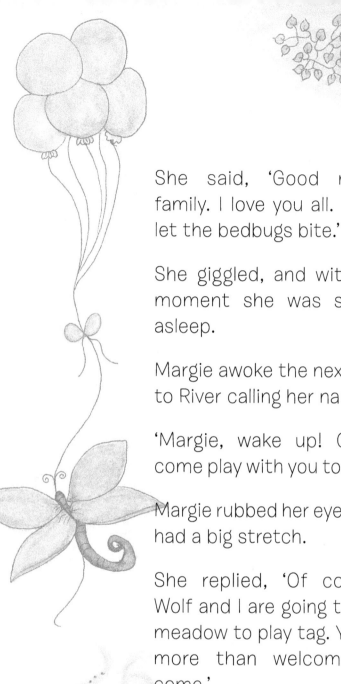

She said, 'Good night, family. I love you all. Don't let the bedbugs bite.'

She giggled, and within a moment she was sound asleep.

Margie awoke the next day to River calling her name.

'Margie, wake up! Can I come play with you today?'

Margie rubbed her eyes and had a big stretch.

She replied, 'Of course. Wolf and I are going to the meadow to play tag. You're more than welcome to come.'

River said, 'Yes, but is there any water near the meadows, for I would have to go for a swim here and there.'

'Yes,' Wolf replied, 'there is a beautiful big stream to play in.'

'Okay, let's go.'

Margie walked out of the cave. She noticed everything was much brighter, and everyone seem to be shining. She rubbed her eyes and took another look but nothing had changed.

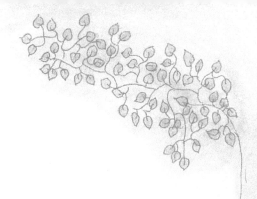

She said to Wolf and River, 'Is everything much brighter today to you?'

They both replied, 'No! It looks like it always does.'

River said, 'It's a beautiful day, isn't it?'

Margie said, 'Yes, everything looks so bright and beautiful.'

She told her mother, who was sitting on the sand with her little sister Pebbles, 'We are going to the meadow to play tag. Is that okay?'

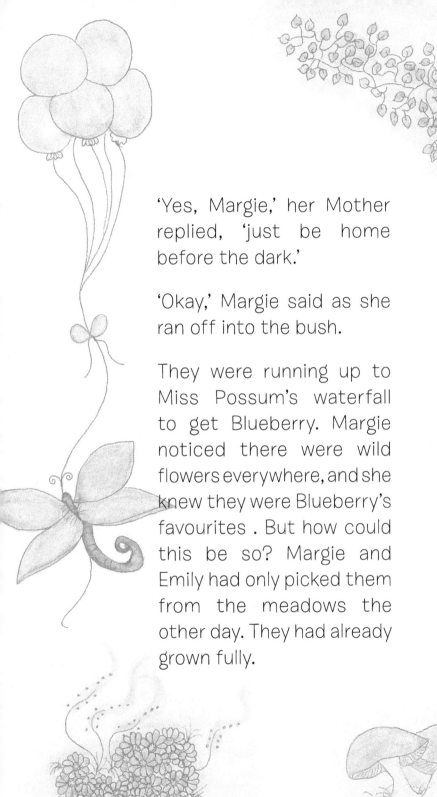

'Yes, Margie,' her Mother replied, 'just be home before the dark.'

'Okay,' Margie said as she ran off into the bush.

They were running up to Miss Possum's waterfall to get Blueberry. Margie noticed there were wild flowers everywhere, and she knew they were Blueberry's favourites . But how could this be so? Margie and Emily had only picked them from the meadows the other day. They had already grown fully.

Margie asked Blueberry, 'Did you use your magic to make the wildflowers grow quicker?'

'No,' Blueberry replied, 'they have just grown like that, all on their own.'

'Oh,' Margie replied, 'well, they do make the waterfall look so much nicer, and it smells so good.'

'I know,' Raspberry replied, 'can we come play tag too?'

'Yes!' Margie said to Raspberry, 'We are meeting some new friends. They are Tree Guardians.'

'Oh, yes, Blueberry told us all about them last night.'

'Yelp,' Margie replied, with a sad face. 'I tried to tell my mother and father, but they didn't believe me.'

'Oh, why?'

'They said Tree Guardians do not exist, and if they did, they would have seen or heard about them from the elders, and since they had never heard of them, they don't believe me.'

'Well, we will just have to work out a way to show them, won't we?' Raspberry replied.

Margie said, 'That's a great idea.'

They all headed towards the meadow. Margie noticed the bush was very bright, and everything was shiny too, but no one else seemed to notice. It was like they saw it this way all the time, so she decided to just enjoy how beautiful everything was. They came across Margie's favourite flowers. They were honey blossoms, and they were all over the place. There were more honey blossom trees than Margie remembered seeing yesterday.

But once again nobody else seemed to notice, so she just enjoyed walking slowly through them. She could feel the softness under her feet as she walked. Then a breeze blew up, and they began to fall from the trees. It was just like when snow falls, but they were the most beautiful pink flowers, and they fell all over Margie. It was such a beautiful moment. Margie just stood still and looked up and watched them fall.

Terrain said, 'Have you ever seen inside a honey blossom tree?'

Margie laughed and said, 'How can you see inside a honey blossom tree? You're being silly now.'

Terrain replied, 'Margie, follow me.'

Right before Margie's eyes appeared a door.

Terrain looked at Margie and said, 'Silly, huh?'

The door opened, and Terrain walked inside. The Berry girls and River followed him straight away, but Margie and Wolf stood and just looked at each other.

Wolf said to Margie, 'Come on. It's a beautiful tree. I don't think there is anything to be scared of.' Then he added, 'I'll go first.'

Wolf walked through the door of the tree, and found there was a very bright light shining inside. Margie, having seen Wolf enter through the door, said to herself, 'It will be okay.'

She took a deep breath and entered the tree too. When she was inside the tree, however, all her friends had disappeared. She turned around, but she could not see anyone. As she began walking backwards, within a moment, she was free-falling. She screamed with fright, and then she landed on a mountain of honey blossom flowers, sunk to the bottom, then she stopped. She stood up to find herself covered in honey blossom flowers. Wolf jumped up and began shaking himself and they began to all get off him. At

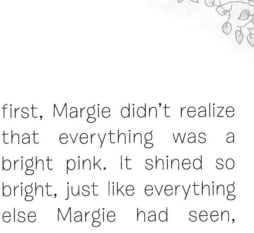

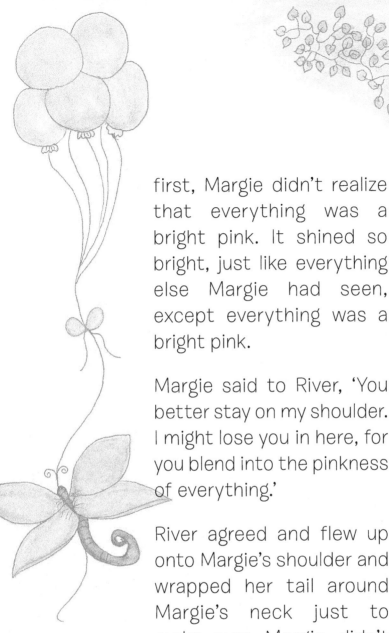

first, Margie didn't realize that everything was a bright pink. It shined so bright, just like everything else Margie had seen, except everything was a bright pink.

Margie said to River, 'You better stay on my shoulder. I might lose you in here, for you blend into the pinkness of everything.'

River agreed and flew up onto Margie's shoulder and wrapped her tail around Margie's neck just to make sure Margie didn't forget her.

Terrain walked over and said, 'Are you all okay?'

They all looked at him and raised their eyebrows.

He looked at them, with his big dopy blue eyes and said, 'Well, it would spoil the fun, if you knew you were going to free fall into a mountain of honey blossom flowers, wouldn't it?'

Margie looked at the others and said, 'Well, yes, if you had of told us that we were going to fall that far, we might have said no!'

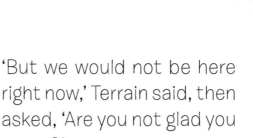

'But we would not be here right now,' Terrain said, then asked, 'Are you not glad you came?'

Margie looked around and said, 'Yep, I'm glad and very happy to be here!'

She walked straight over to a pink mango tree and picked a fruit and began to eat it.

'Yummy,' she said, and then she asked Terrain, 'But why is everything pink?'

Terrain just smiled and shrugged his shoulders.

Blueberry said, 'Is that a pink banana tree?'

Terrain nodded his head and said, 'Yep! That's what it is.'

Margie noticed it was the bush inside the honey blossom tree. But everything was pink and shiny and much prettier. Even Wolf and the Berry girls were all pink—everything was pink.

Terrain said, 'Let's go to the meadows. My sisters are waiting for us. Follow me!'

He went down a hole and slid up. Then they were in the middle of the meadows. They began to sing and skip over to Keenly and Indigo.

Margie saw from the corner of her eye a Wolf hiding behind the trees. She went to ask Wolf if he was playing hide and go seek, when Wolf ran past her. Margie realized it was not Wolf she saw. Then she ran as fast as she could to catch up to Wolf. When she caught up, she saw a pack of wolves playing, and Wolf was one of them. It was hard to tell which one was Wolf, for they all were grey and white. Once they stopped, Wolf ran straight up to Margie and the other wolves followed him.

Wolf said, 'This is my pack, Margie, and these are my brothers.'

Margie's heart stopped! A lump went up to her throat.

'Hello, nice to meet you all,' she said.

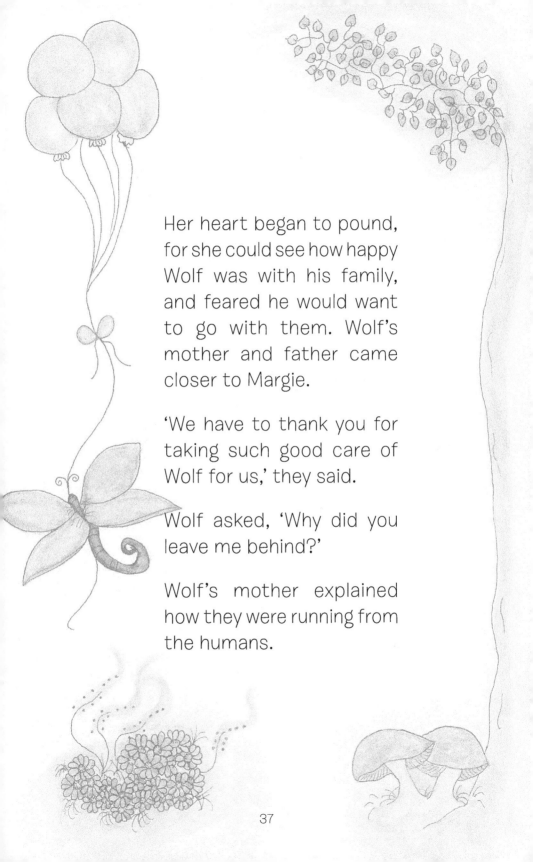

Her heart began to pound, for she could see how happy Wolf was with his family, and feared he would want to go with them. Wolf's mother and father came closer to Margie.

'We have to thank you for taking such good care of Wolf for us,' they said.

Wolf asked, 'Why did you leave me behind?'

Wolf's mother explained how they were running from the humans.

Wolf's father said, 'You were so small, Wolf, and could not keep up. We lost you. So when I went back to find you, you were playing with the little girl, and I knew you would be safe with her. The humans were heading straight for you, so I began to howl to lead them away from you both.'

Wolf looked at Margie, and Margie smiled at him.

'See? I told you there would be a good reason why,' she said.

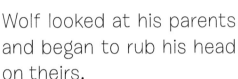

Wolf looked at his parents and began to rub his head on theirs.

Wolf's mother said, 'We always come back every spring to check on you. It's just you have such a beautiful bond with Margie. We never wanted you to have make you choice between Margie and us. But we have always dreamed of you one day joining us again.'

Margie's smile left her face, and her heart began to race. Wolf could hear and see Margie's fear and quickly put her mind at rest.

He said, 'My tribe is my pack now. I could never leave them. They are my family.'

Wolf's parents said to him, 'Yes! We see that. That's why we have never asked this of you before, but we just had to make sure you knew in your heart that we wanted you with us.'

Margie's heart began to slow down, and she took a deep breath.

The wolf pack began to leave; his parents started to rub their head on Wolf. Margie felt a tear fall down her cheek, for she knew Wolf's heart would be breaking. It doesn't matter who your family is. It's always hard to say goodbye. There is an invisible bond that connects us that can only be felt in our hearts. Sometimes, it's happy and makes you feel safe. And sometimes, it's sad and makes you feel hurt. Today was both for Wolf. As Wolf's parents began to leave, Margie looked straight into Wolf's eyes.

'Are you sure you don't want to go? I know there must be a part of you that wants to be with your pack.'

Wolf looked at his parents and then looked at Margie.

He said, 'Margie, a part of me will always want to run free with my pack, of course. But I would never be happy if you were not running beside me.'

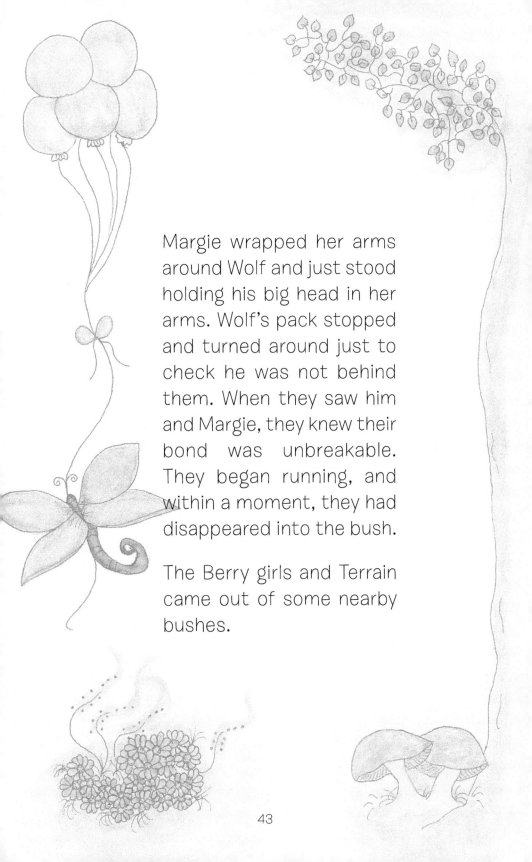

Margie wrapped her arms around Wolf and just stood holding his big head in her arms. Wolf's pack stopped and turned around just to check he was not behind them. When they saw him and Margie, they knew their bond was unbreakable. They began running, and within a moment, they had disappeared into the bush.

The Berry girls and Terrain came out of some nearby bushes.

'Wow! Are you two okay?'

Margie looked at Wolf and waited for his reply.

Wolf said, 'Yep, I will race you to the other side of the meadows,' and he took off as fast as he could.

The others began to laugh and run behind him. Margie was running. She noticed everything was still shining, and when she would touch the trees or flowers, as she ran through them, the brightness would become big and bright, but still no one else seemed to notice it. Margie scratched her head and called out to Wolf.

'Does the bush seem different to you today?'

Wolf stopped and looked at Margie.

'What do you mean different, Margie?'

Margie said, 'Oh, don't worry. It must be me. My eyes are a little bit blurry today. That's all.'

She kept running until she got to the other side of the meadows.

Keenly and Indigo came running up to them and said, 'What has taken you so long?'

'Well,' Terrain said, 'I kind of showed Margie what it's like inside a honey blossom tree, and Wolf met his pack for the first time since he was a pup, so it took a little bit longer to get here.'

'Oh! Okay,' Keenly said.

Then Indigo asked Wolf, 'What was it like to meet your family?'

'Well,' Wolf replied, 'I don't remember them from when I was a pup, so it was like I was meeting them for the first time. And it was really good to see what my parents were like. I look just like my father. And now I know I didn't do anything wrong for them to leave me behind. They left me behind because they loved me.'

Everyone was happy for Wolf.

When Margie looked around, she saw all her friends had come to play too. There was Bobby and Joey, Willow, and even Willy wagtail came to play. Mr Platypus, Cooper, and Mr Frog were watching from the stream. The game was about to start. They all stood in a circle and did one potato, two potato, until someone was in. And this time, it was Margie.

'Okay,' she said, 'take sides!'

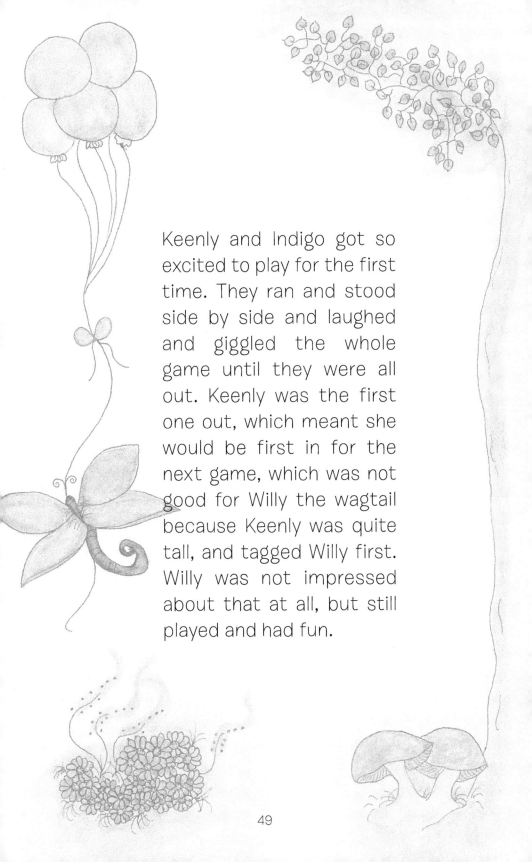

Keenly and Indigo got so excited to play for the first time. They ran and stood side by side and laughed and giggled the whole game until they were all out. Keenly was the first one out, which meant she would be first in for the next game, which was not good for Willy the wagtail because Keenly was quite tall, and tagged Willy first. Willy was not impressed about that at all, but still played and had fun.

Once they had played a few games, they all went over to the stream to see their old friends. They sat down at the edge of the stream with their feet in the water, talking to Mr Platypus and Mr Frog, who were happy and enjoyed the company.

Cooper said to Blueberry, 'How have you been? We do miss you and Gully very much. It's a bit quiet around here now you have gone.'

Miss Firefly said, 'We do miss hearing you sing.'

'Oh,' Blueberry said, 'I do think of you all the time and wonder how you're going since it was such a very hot the summer this year.'

Mr Frog said, 'Yes, hot! It was indeed, but we did get some rain, and the stream kept us cool.'

Blueberry asked, 'What's your favourite song? And we will sing it for you.'

Mr Frog said, 'Our favourite song is the water song, "Where you stay all day."'

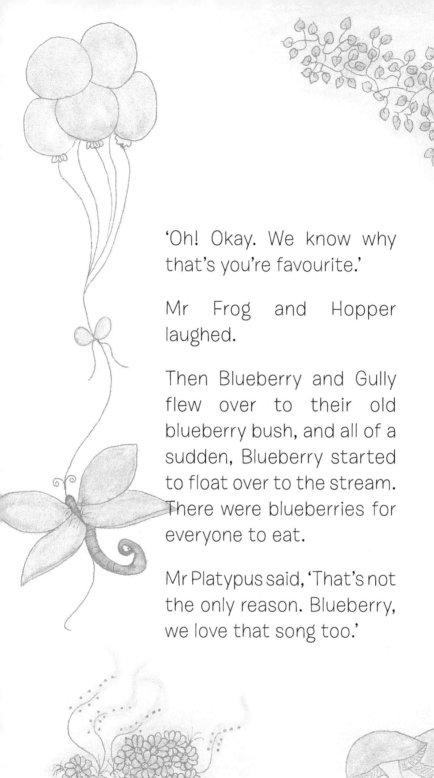

'Oh! Okay. We know why that's you're favourite.'

Mr Frog and Hopper laughed.

Then Blueberry and Gully flew over to their old blueberry bush, and all of a sudden, Blueberry started to float over to the stream. There were blueberries for everyone to eat.

Mr Platypus said, 'That's not the only reason. Blueberry, we love that song too.'

'Oh, I know that silly, but we know it's a little bit why you love that song.' Said Blueberry.

'Yes, well, it's a little bit why,' he replied, as they all started to eat the blueberries.

Blueberry and Gully got ready to sing.

Miss Firefly flew up and said, 'Now I would like to introduce you all to Blueberry and her very best friend Gully to sing their song.

A buss a buss a
buss, buss, buss,
To the edge of the
water is where we play,
for summer time is here,
And it's quite hot today.
Gully said to me:
A buss, a buss, a
buss, buss, buss,
I am going to the
water to play,
I am going to stay all day,
Until the sun has
gone away.

A buss, a buss, a
buss, buss, buss,
Another day, where
time is the gift.
It's a gift and a treat
for Gully and me,
With nothing much
else to do;
For we are free, to
do what we please,
For we live in a
blueberry tree.

A buss, a buss, a
buss, buss, buss,
For our friends are
waiting for us,
At the edge of the water,
And then they pop their
heads up and say,
Have you brought some
yummy blueberries
for us today? As
gully said,
A buss a buss, a
buss, buss, buss,
Of course, we have,
for we know
how much you
love them, hey!

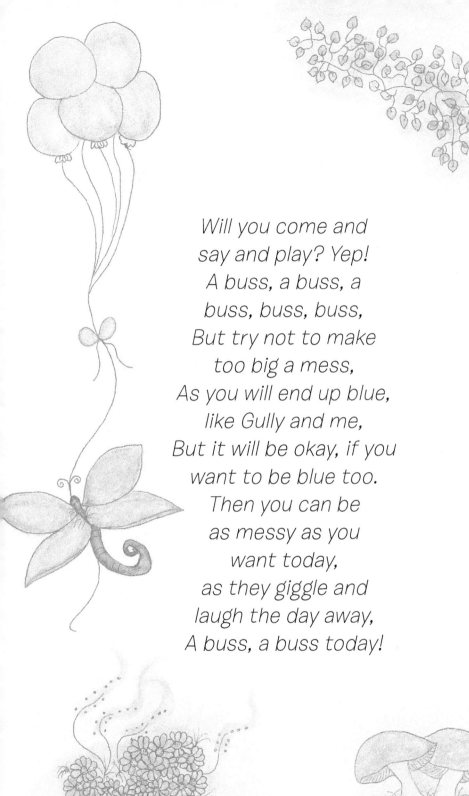

Will you come and
say and play? Yep!
A buss, a buss, a
buss, buss, buss,
But try not to make
too big a mess,
As you will end up blue,
like Gully and me,
But it will be okay, if you
want to be blue too.
Then you can be
as messy as you
want today,
as they giggle and
laugh the day away,
A buss, a buss today!

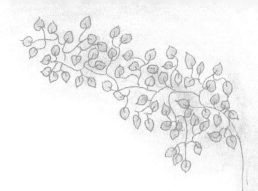

Margie laughed, as she remembered that day: Jasper caught her eating blueberries when she was not supposed to, and her face was blue instead of brown. It seemed like such a long time ago.

Margie took some Blueberries over to Terrace. She called out, 'Terrace, I have

a surprise for you.'

Terrace looked down and then slowly made his way down from the tree.

'Oh, thank you,' he said to Margie.

Margie replied, 'You're welcome. Do you want to come play?'

'Oh, no! I am a bit sleepily today. I will just watch from up in my tree.'

'Oh, Terrace, you're always asleep.'

Terrace said, 'You just don't understand.'

He climbed back up his tree
and started to sing a song
to Margie. Margie waved for
the others to come over to
listen.

My Yummy Gum Leaves
As the day starts, I
wake to the smell
Of fresh yummy
gummy leaves,
Just sitting there
waiting for me.
I live in a tree,
way up high,

I can see my friend's
playing below,
From the corner
of my eyes.
Yummy gummy
leaves for me,
I sleep in the shade
of the big gum tree.
Come and play, my
friends say to me.
But I say, 'Oh,
maybe later,
I am a bit sleepily
I will just watch
You all from up here.'

Yummy gummy
leaves for me,
As they play hide
and go seek.
Willow is in, she
will find you,
And she will find
me, but for now,
I will sleep and
dream of places
I've never been, and
one day hope to see.

But for now, I will
sit high up
In my big gum tree,
eating and saying:
Yummy gummy
leaves for me,
I can watch the sunsets
come and go,
I can eat yummy
gummy leaves
all day if I please, for
this is the life for me.

My name Terrace,
and this is where
you can find me:
just look up,
in the big shaded
gum tree.

Margie said, 'Now, I understand you just love living in the trees.'

Terrace said, 'Yes, this is the life for me. I do love watching you all from up here in

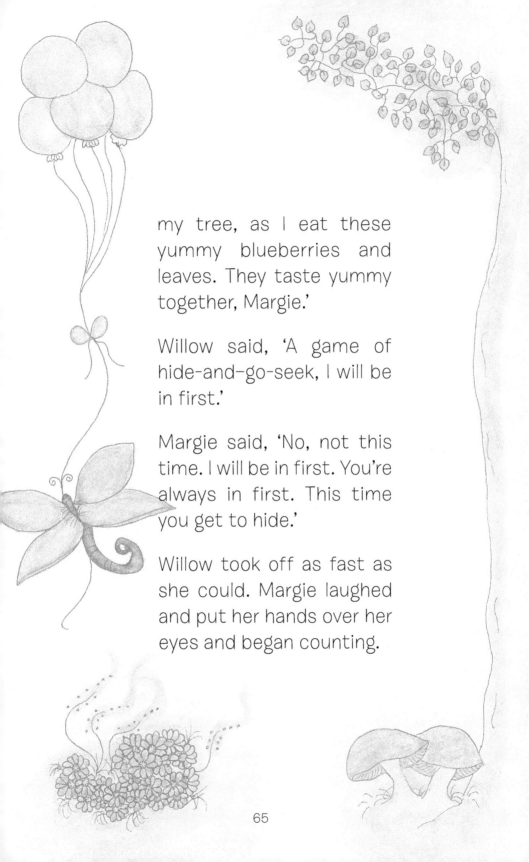

my tree, as I eat these yummy blueberries and leaves. They taste yummy together, Margie.'

Willow said, 'A game of hide-and-go-seek, I will be in first.'

Margie said, 'No, not this time. I will be in first. You're always in first. This time you get to hide.'

Willow took off as fast as she could. Margie laughed and put her hands over her eyes and began counting.

Finally, she said, 'Ready or not, here I come!'

Margie looked under the logs, behind the trees.

'Where are you?' she yelled, as she ran around looking everywhere.

She went over to the stream. Mr Frog pointed over behind the rocks. Then Margie tip-toed over to find them all sitting, eating blueberries, and giggling with blue faces and blue hands. The only one who was not there was Willow.

Margie said, 'Oh, my goodness, you all need a wash.'

Mr Frog said, 'Oh, no! Not in my stream.'

But Blueberry said to him, 'Do you not want to have beautiful blue water?'

'Well, when you say it like that.'

Keenly said, 'And your stream will smell of blueberries.'

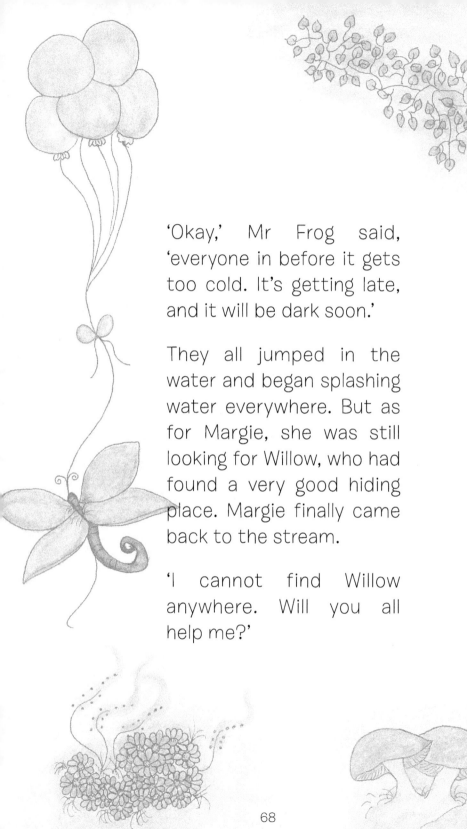

'Okay,' Mr Frog said, 'everyone in before it gets too cold. It's getting late, and it will be dark soon.'

They all jumped in the water and began splashing water everywhere. But as for Margie, she was still looking for Willow, who had found a very good hiding place. Margie finally came back to the stream.

'I cannot find Willow anywhere. Will you all help me?'

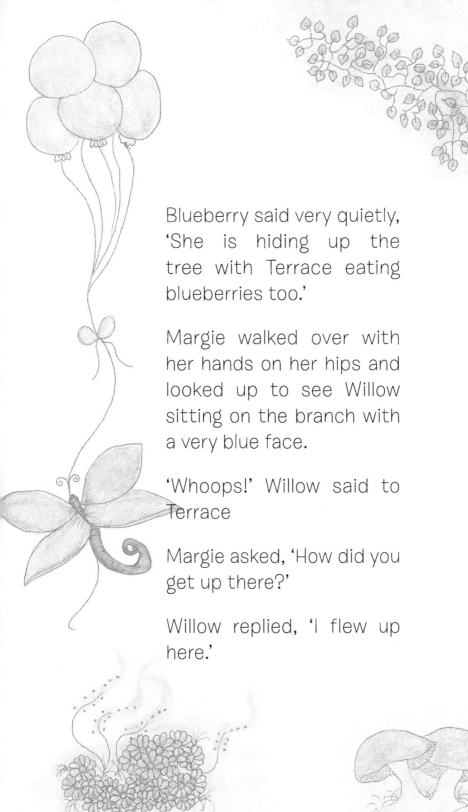

Blueberry said very quietly,
'She is hiding up the
tree with Terrace eating
blueberries too.'

Margie walked over with
her hands on her hips and
looked up to see Willow
sitting on the branch with
a very blue face.

'Whoops!' Willow said to
Terrace

Margie asked, 'How did you
get up there?'

Willow replied, 'I flew up
here.'

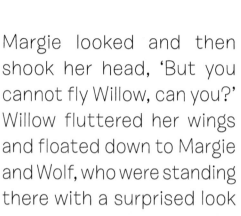

Margie looked and then shook her head, 'But you cannot fly Willow, can you?' Willow fluttered her wings and floated down to Margie and Wolf, who were standing there with a surprised look on their face.

'Well,' Margie said, 'that was a very good place to hide, Willow.'

Willow said, 'I thought you had found me quite a few times, but you just kept on walking under the tree and didn't look up.'

'Well,' Margie said, 'I didn't think in my wildest dreams. I would never see an emu sitting in a tree. I said to Mr Frog, I cannot find them anywhere!'

They all laughed and jumped in the stream.

Then Margie said to the others, 'One more game of tag so we can all dry off.'

They all ran over to the meadow for one last game.

Wolf yelled, 'Last one there is in'

They all ran as fast as they could. The last one there was Emily.

'Oh dear,' she said, 'this game could take a while because I am a bit slow.'

Wolf said, 'I will help you.'

Emily said, 'Yes! Let's go.'

One, two, three and a couple more, and they were all out, and it was time to make their way back to the waterfall. The sun began to fade. Margie noticed that everything had turn orange instead of pink. The sky had become a deep red. She had never seen it that colour before.

She said to the others, 'The sky is very red.'

They all looked up at the sky and then looked at Margie.

'Yes, hmm... it's a bit red today,' they said, and continued walking.

Margie looked at the others and noticed that no one else seemed to care, so she just kept on walking. They all waved goodbye to their friends that live in the meadows. Margie noticed Terrain, Indigo, and Keenly were not coming.

She ran up to them and said, 'Why are you not coming?'

'Oh,' Terrain said, 'we will stay here for the night. This is where Momma and Father will come for us.'

'Okay,' Margie replied, 'can you ask your mom and father if you can come to the waterfall tomorrow?'

'Yes!' Keenly replied, then added, 'Thank you for letting us play today. It was a very fun day.'

'You're welcome, my new friends.'

Margie waved goodbye and said, 'Maybe we will see you tomorrow.'

She crossed her fingers and ran to the others.

Blueberry said, 'We will come back soon to visit Mr Frog, Mr Platypus, Cooper and Miss Firefly.'

They all nodded their heads and waved goodbye. They all ran home to Miss Possum's waterfall as fast as they could. They were running when Margie stopped and noticed that Wolf was not running beside her. She turned and followed her feet back the way she came to find him lying near the bush, where his parents were watching them from. She looked to see the honey blossom trees that were nearby and decided to go have a closer look to see if she could find the doorway in again. But it seemed to have disappeared. It didn't matter where Margie looked, she could not find it. Wolf walked over to see what she was doing.

He asked, 'Margie, what are you looking for?'

Margie replied, 'The door that was here earlier.'

Wolf looked at her and said, 'The door to the tree?'

'Yes! You know the door that Terrain showed us. On the way to the Meadow, I am sure this is the tree.'

Wolf said to Margie, 'Come! I think it's time we should go home.'

Margie looked at Wolf and said, 'Hmm . . . I suppose so.'

As they were walking, Margie asked Wolf, 'What were you doing back there?'

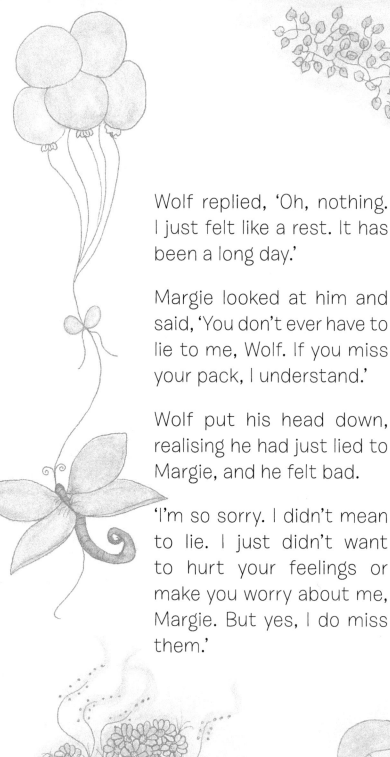

Wolf replied, 'Oh, nothing. I just felt like a rest. It has been a long day.'

Margie looked at him and said, 'You don't ever have to lie to me, Wolf. If you miss your pack, I understand.'

Wolf put his head down, realising he had just lied to Margie, and he felt bad.

'I'm so sorry. I didn't mean to lie. I just didn't want to hurt your feelings or make you worry about me, Margie. But yes, I do miss them.'

Margie said, 'You know, I only ever want you to be happy Wolf, even if that means letting you go free to be with your pack. As sad as I would be, I would miss you very much. If that was where you're truly happy and wanted to be, then that's where you should be, Wolf!'

'Oh, Margie,' Wolf replied, 'I said I missed them, but I could never live without you. You're my family. I just wanted to get their scent that's all.'

'Oh!' Margie smiled and said, 'you know even though I said all that, I was just pretending. I would have been very sad if you had of lefted to go with his pack.'

'I know that, Margie. I could hear your sadness and smell your fear. I am a wolf, and that's one of my gifts.'

Margie laughed and cuddled Wolf and said, 'I love you very much.'

She knew in her heart that he was sad. Wolf pushed Margie from behind gently.

Margie said, 'You know you love me too.'

Wolf snuggled up close to her. Then they walked back to the beach. Once they got there, they sat and looked up at the sky. It was still the prettiest red.

Margie said to Wolf once again, 'The sky is very red tonight.'

Wolf looked at Margie and said, 'Yes! It's beautiful. Even the stars are brighter tonight.'

Margie replied. 'Yes, there are lots of stars out tonight. It's a bit unusual. Tonight there looks to be so many more stars out there as they fade in and out of the redness. I have never seen the night sky look as beautiful as it does tonight.'

Wolf started to touch Margie with his nose, and she began to laugh.

'Stop it! Your nose is very cold and wet, Wolf.'

Wolf howled and began to sing the most beautiful song to Margie of how he really felt about the special bond he had with her.

Going Back in Time

I am a wolf, and
I live a life
where I am free to
do as I please.
If I could go back in time
and change the path
that's now mine,
I would say no!
For where I live today,
I am happy and
don't mind.

If I could go back in time,
would I change my mind?
I would say No!
For I love my life.
If I could go back in time
and change the path
that's now mine,
I would say No!

My footsteps would be
in the same place
they were
the last time.
For freedom for my
body and soul
is why I have come
back this time.

I might have to
follow my feet
more than a few times.
If I could go back in time
and change the path
that's now mine,
I would say no!
For the journey
and the choices
have always been
all mine.

And I don't mind,
for our footsteps
are forever and will
always entwine

Until the end of time.
And no! I don't mind.
If I could go back in time,
would I change the path
that's now yours
and mine?
I would say no!

For my journey
through this life
I would always want
you by my side.
A thousand sunrises
and sunsets,
they are all yours
and mine.

If I could go back in time
And change the journey
that has become
yours and mine,
I would say No!

And no, I don't mind.
I am glad my footsteps
stopped by your side.
If I could go back
in time?
That does not ever
enter my mind.
Our lives will always
be entwined.

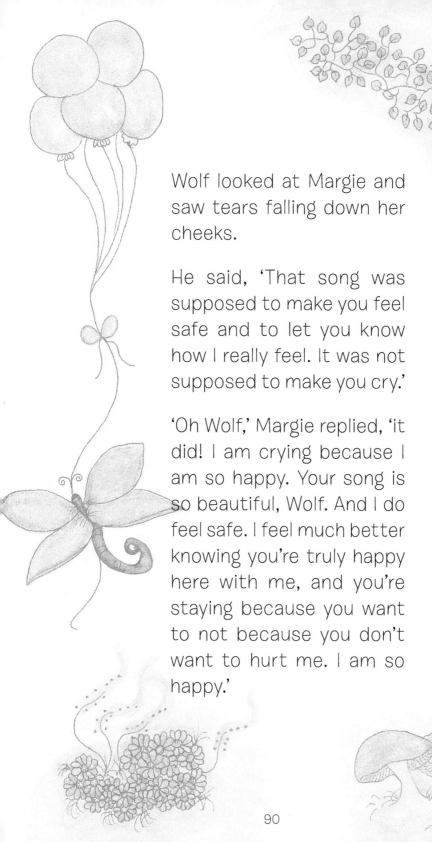

Wolf looked at Margie and saw tears falling down her cheeks.

He said, 'That song was supposed to make you feel safe and to let you know how I really feel. It was not supposed to make you cry.'

'Oh Wolf,' Margie replied, 'it did! I am crying because I am so happy. Your song is so beautiful, Wolf. And I do feel safe. I feel much better knowing you're truly happy here with me, and you're staying because you want to not because you don't want to hurt me. I am so happy.'

She began to cry even harder and cuddle Wolf.

Once Margie stopped crying, she asked wolf, 'Well, what do you want to do?'

'Hmm...' Wolf replied, 'let's go see what's happening at Miss Possum's waterfall.'

Margie said, 'I will race you.'

Wolf replied, 'No, it's a beautiful night. Let's just walk.'

Margie put her hand on Wolf's back and said, 'Okay.'

When they got to the waterfall, everyone was lying down just gazing at the stars and saying how beautiful the night sky was.

Margie said, 'I have never seen the sky this red as it was tonight.'

Miss Possum said, 'It's always that red colour when the seasons are changing.'

Margie looked at Wolf and said, 'Oh that's why.'

Margie looked up at Terrace's tree to see Terrain looking down at them.

She sat up and said, 'Hello, what are you doing all the way up there?'

'Oh,' Terrain replied, 'not a lot, just hanging around.'

Miss Possum and all the others sat up to meet Terrain, for they had heard of Tree Guardians but had never seen or met one before.

Terrain came down and sat next to Margie and Wolf, and he said to Wolf, 'Was that your family today?'

Everyone's ears stood up to listen.

'Yes,' Wolf replied.

Terrain asked, 'You know, they come quite often to see you and check you're okay.'

Margie and Wolf looked at Terrain.

Then Margie said, 'What do you mean they come quite often?'

Terrain replied, 'Well, that's not the first time I have seen them watching you. Now I realise, Wolf is one of the pack.'

Wolf replied, 'Yes, they are my pack.'

Blueberry looked at wolf and said, 'But you're not going to leave us, are you?'

'No!' Wolf replied, 'You cannot get rid of me that easily.'

Blueberry flew up to Wolf and kissed him on his nose and said, 'I would be very sad if you went away, Wolf.'

Then she laughed and said, 'You have a very wet nose, Wolf,' and wiped her mouth. The others all laughed and were very happy. Wolf had decided to stay with them.

Jillian fluttered over to see what was going on. Margie held her hand out, and Jillian landed on it.

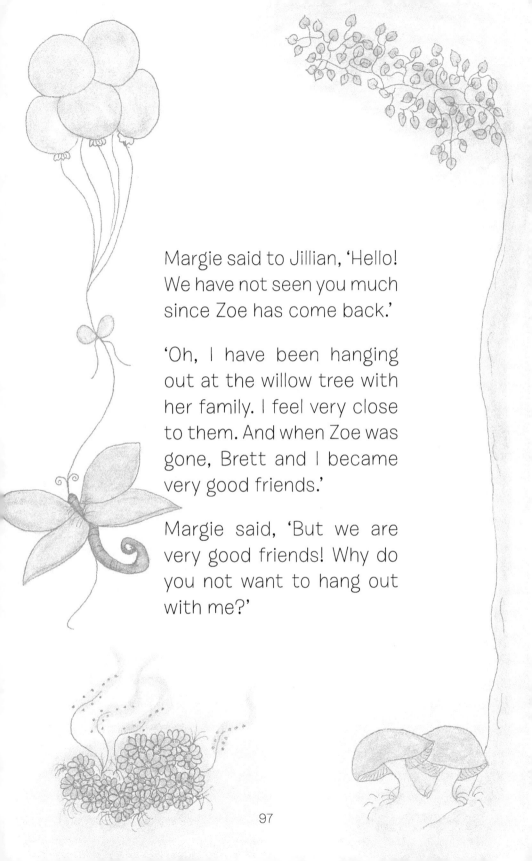

Margie said to Jillian, 'Hello! We have not seen you much since Zoe has come back.'

'Oh, I have been hanging out at the willow tree with her family. I feel very close to them. And when Zoe was gone, Brett and I became very good friends.'

Margie said, 'But we are very good friends! Why do you not want to hang out with me?'

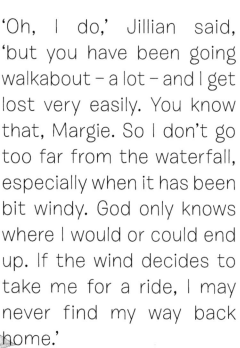

'Oh, I do,' Jillian said, 'but you have been going walkabout – a lot – and I get lost very easily. You know that, Margie. So I don't go too far from the waterfall, especially when it has been bit windy. God only knows where I would or could end up. If the wind decides to take me for a ride, I may never find my way back home.'

They all roared with laughter at the way Jillian said it and how big her eyes became with the thought of getting lost again. Jillian even laughed at herself.

Margie piped up and said, 'Well, we will play at the waterfall tomorrow. Do you want to stay and play with us?'

Jillian replied, 'Of course, that sounds like fun.'

Margie said, 'We have to go. It has been a very long day, and it's time for sleep.'

Wolf got up, and Terrain said to Margie, 'Can I come back to the waterfall and play tomorrow too?'

'Yes, Terrain, you don't have to ask. You're welcome to come and play any time you like.'

'Okay,' he said, and in a second, he was gone. Margie and Wolf waved goodbye to the others and said, 'We will see you all too tomorrow.'

They slowly made their way back into their cave. Margie began to tell her mother about Terrain again, but Margie's mother still didn't believe in Tree Guardians.

Margie said to Wolf, 'Well, she will be surprised tomorrow when we bring Terrain to meet her, won't she?'

Wolf mourned and laid his head on Margie's belly, and off to sleep he went. Margie laid, staring at the fireflies above, as she stroked Wolf's fur, thinking of Wolf's pack and what she would have done if he had decided to go with his pack and how everything would be so different without him. The days would be very long and Margie thought about how lonely she would be without Wolf, as she pulled her head up to look at him. It had been a long day for

him, and he was sound asleep—and was snoring quite loudly. Margie giggled to herself, and off to sleep she went too.

The sun was rising, and Father had gone to catch the fish for dinner. Mother was on the beach with Pebbles. And the rest of the tribe had set out to find fruit for the day. Jasper was collecting twigs for the fire to cook the fish on. River swam up to the sand, to Margie's mother.

'Where's Margie?' she asked.

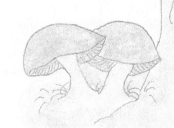

Mother replied, 'She is being a sleepy head, and she and Wolf are still asleep in the cave.'

'Thank you!,' River replied, 'I will go and wake them up. We have a big day planned. We are going to the meadows.'

She flew up and into the cave.

'Margie! Margie! Wake up.'

Wolf opened his eyes to see River, and she said, 'Let's go!' Then Margie opened one of her eyes.

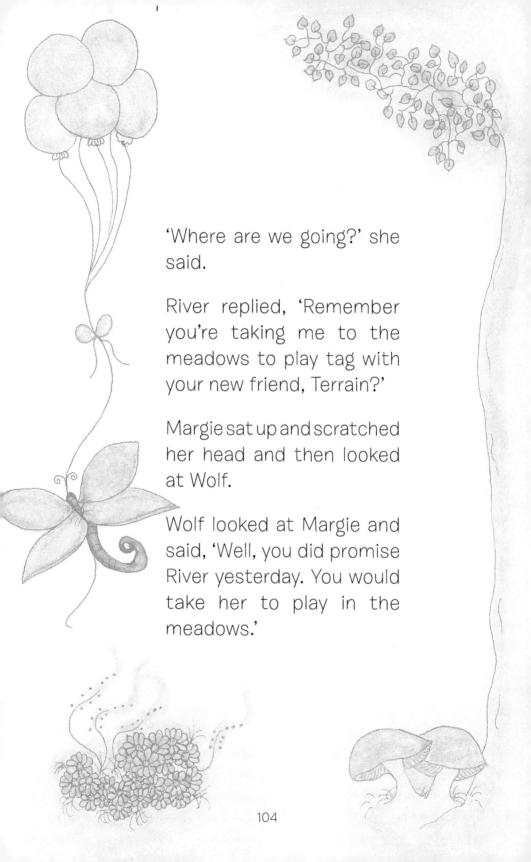

'Where are we going?' she said.

River replied, 'Remember you're taking me to the meadows to play tag with your new friend, Terrain?'

Margie sat up and scratched her head and then looked at Wolf.

Wolf looked at Margie and said, 'Well, you did promise River yesterday. You would take her to play in the meadows.'

Margie shook her head and said, 'But we have already been to the meadows yesterday, and we played with Terrain. Remember? Blueberry came too, to say hello to Mr Frog and all the gang at the stream.'

Wolf and River started to laugh. 'No, that's today, Margie. We are going to the meadows today.'

'No,' Margie said, 'we went yesterday.'

Margie's Mother came in and said, 'Well, are you all going to the meadows or are you going to just sit around here all day? Or are you going to play with your new imaginary new friends you were telling us all about last night? Grandfather said that when he woke up, you have the best imagination in the bush, Margie.'

Margie got up and walked outside.

She said to Wolf, 'How are you feeling?'

Wolf looked at Margie and said, 'I'm fine, Margie. How are you feeling?'

'Well, I'm not sure,' Margie replied. 'Are you sure we didn't go to the meadows yesterday and play tag with Keenly and Indigo?'

'No, Margie,' Wolf replied, 'that's today.'

And right in that moment, Margie realised it was all a dream. That's why everything was so much brighter, and the sky was so red. Maybe the wolf pack would be out there today. Margie's heart started to race, in the thought that if they were, maybe Wolf would go with them.

Wolf looked at Margie and said, 'Margie! You have gone very pale. Here, you better sit down.'

Margie sat down on the soft sand. Her first thought was, "If I don't go to the meadow and if Wolf's pack is out there, he will not see them, and I will not have to worry about him leaving." And then she remembered how at peace he was when he found out why they had left him. She knew, right then, she had to go to the meadows today.

She said, 'Let's go and see if the Berry girls want to come.'

They ran up to Miss Possum's waterfall.

'Girls!' Margie called. 'We are going to the meadows to play tag. Do you want to come?'

She hoped that Raspberry and Blackberry would say yes, for that meant that the dream would be different, and then she would have nothing to worry about, but just like it was in her dream, Blueberry was the only one that came out of Miss Possum's cave and said, 'I will, but the other girls are staying with Mother for the day.'

Margie knew right then that Wolf was going to meet his parents today.

She looked at Wolf and said, 'Are you ready? Wolf, are you ready for a great day?'

Wolf replied, 'Yes, let's go!'

They set out for the meadow, just like in Margie's dream. Terrain was waiting near the honey blossom tree. And he said, 'Do you want to come in and see what a honey blossom tree looks like on the inside?'

Margie looked at Wolf and said, 'No, not today! We are just going to sit and have a rest beneath the honey blossom tree today.'

River said to Margie, 'Are you a bit sick today?'

Margie just looked at her and said, 'No, I am waiting for someone.'

They sat down.

Wolf asked Margie, 'Who are we waiting for?'

Out from the bushes came Wolf's pack. Wolf looked at Margie, and she smiled at him.

'I will always love you. No matter where you are. It's time for you to go with your pack and be a wolf for a while. I will be here when you get back.'

Margie said to the others, 'Let's go to the meadows.'

She ran off, for she knew in her dream that Wolf only stayed because of her, and she knew his heart was really with his pack. She wanted him to be truly happy, so she set him free.

Mythical Books & Designs

CPSIA information can be obtained
at www.ICGtesting.com
Printed in the USA
BVHW031015050419
544725BV00001B/86/P